* Bad * CAT * Good CAT *

First published in 2011 by HarperCollins *Children's Books*
HarperCollins *Children's Books* is a division of HarperCollins*Publishers* Ltd
77-85 Fulham Palace Road, Hammersmith, London W6 8JB

Visit us on the web at www.harpercollins.co.uk

1 3 5 7 9 8 6 4 2

ISBN: 978-0-00-741904-3

Printed and bound in Great Britain by
Clays Ltd, St Ives plc

Bad Cat

Lynne Reid Banks
Illustrated by Tony Ross

Good Cat

HarperCollins *Children's Books*

For Paloma and David.

Naturally.

1. Cat-Crazy

This is the story of two families, two children and two cats. Of course, the cats are by far the most important.

As you'll know, if you happen to have a cat in your family, every cat behaves as if he or she were the king or queen of the house. Cats aren't there for people,

people are there for cats. And the first cat in my story *definitely* believed that that was the way things should be.

The first thing to say about this cat is that he was bad. I can't easily tell you what a bad, bad cat he was. But I'm going to try. Because, although he was bad, I like him. And so did David. He was David's cat. Well... David was his person.

A word about David.

David was crazy about cats. He'd always watched movies about cats, starting with *Tom and Jerry*. He'd seen *The Aristocats* too many times to count, and more recently he'd been given a DVD of a Japanese film with warrior cats who wore armour and fought with swords. The film was all in Japanese but David didn't care. He made up what they were saying to each other, and

dreamed of having a Wii of it so he could practise sword-fighting, cat-hero-style.

He shared all this with Paloma, the girl who lived next door to him. Paloma was the same age as him. They were friends for one main reason: they were both cat-crazy. Her favourite books were *Slinky Malinki* and *Orlando the Marmalade Cat.*

David was more into serious books about cats. He really knew a lot about them; about where different kinds of cat

came from, and how in Egypt people thought they were gods while in England some people thought they weren't gods at all, but devils and witches' helpers.

He found all this wonderfully exciting, and it was very good for his reading. These books were quite grown-up and had long words in them. But that was good too, because David and Paloma collected words, and especially cat-words. His favourite at the moment was 'cat-aclysm', but he also liked 'cat-acomb'. He knew what they meant, too (something very bad happening to a cat, and an underground place for dead cats).

On birthdays he often got given books about cats. But as his next birthday came close, his parents asked him an important question.

"You can choose between two big

presents," his dad said. "One is a Wii."

A Wii! His dream! He couldn't imagine anything he'd like better.

"Oh, yes, please!" he said excitedly.

"Well, but wait. The other thing you might want is a cat."

David stood there, his mouth open. He'd asked for a cat so often, and the answer had always been No.

"A real cat?"

"Yes. We think you're old enough now to take care of it."

David was speechless. A cat was something he felt he didn't just *want*. He needed it. The Wii of his dreams just floated away. From then till his birthday, all he dreamed about was his cat that was coming.

2. A Bad Cat Arrives

The cat arrived on his birthday.

When David first saw him, he was so happy he couldn't move or speak. He just stood there gazing. Out of the carry-box came a snow-white cat with long, silky fur. He stalked out of the little gate, his tail unfolded and stuck up straight. When

he saw David, he stood still and gazed back. He had *blue eyes.*

He was the most beautiful creature David had ever seen.

"Are you pleased with him?" his dad asked.

David shook his head. Shaking your head usually means no, but in this case it meant, "I'm so pleased I don't know what to say." He just silently hugged his mum and then his dad and then bent down, picked up the cat, and tried to hug him too.

Now, I'm not going to start making excuses for this cat. But David just might have hugged him too tight. In any case, the cat reached up a pawful of claws and scratched David on the nose. (I did tell you he was bad.)

"OW!" shouted David, and dropped

him. This didn't bother the cat, who landed on all four feet and began to run round and round the living room like a mad thing.

All three of them tried to catch him, but he was too quick for them. He was like a streak of white lightning. When they cornered him near the window, he leaped up on to the sofa, and then on to anarmchair, and from the back of that, on to the mantelpiece.

His long fluffy tail was switching dangerously. It knocked over a vase, which fell to the floor and smashed into a hundred bits. Don't even ask about the water and flowers that were in it.

David's mum was very upset. "Oh, you bad cat!" she cried.

The noise of the crash had upset the cat too. When she reached for him, he

thought, *I'm for it! She's going to hit me!*

He put his ears back, his mouth made a pink diamond, and he looked like a snake. He hissed. If she hadn't backed off, he'd have bitten her.

David thought he was magnificent, like a little tiger, or one of the god-cats in Egyptian wall paintings.

"Shhhhh, shhhhh!" said David. "Don't be angry!" He reached up and lifted the cat off the mantelpiece. (The cat knew at once that this one wasn't going to hit him.) David stroked his fur gently. "I'm going to take you to meet Paloma," he said.

David's dad said, "Be careful he doesn't run away."

David looked at him in horror. "Run away? Why should he?"

"Just be careful. If you're going out the front, keep hold of him. He doesn't know that he lives here yet."

3. Paloma Feels Funny

David carefully carried the cat out to the road and down the path leading to Paloma's house.

A word about Paloma.

Paloma didn't collect dolls. Just soft-toy cats. They all had names and they all had different personalities. She played

endless games with them.

She couldn't persuade David to play with her toy cats, but they talked cats whenever they met. David told her lots of interesting facts about cats from his books, and they collected cat words together. Paloma liked 'cat-alogue' (a book that listed cats), 'cat-aract' (a waterfall made of cats) and 'cat-erpillar' (a pillar shaped like a cat). She liked drawing these last two.

Her un-favourite cat word was 'cat-erwaul', which means loud cat-like crying. She didn't like that one because her dad sometimes said she was doing it when really she was just having a little cry, like you do.

When the doorbell rang, she ran to answer it. She knew it was David because he had a special ring. *Ding...*

ding-ding-diiiing. She was glad it was him, but when she opened the door, she got a shock.

There in his arms was the most beautiful cat she'd ever seen.

"Is... is it yours?" she asked.

"Yes! He's my best birthday present!" said David. She had never seen him looking so happy.

And no wonder, she thought. White. Fluffy. Blue eyes. A real, real cat. And so special!

Paloma didn't say anything. She had a funny feeling. You can probably guess what it was. She had to bite her lip to keep the feeling inside. She reached out her hand and stroked the white cat. It had the softest fur, softer than any of her toy cats.

"I want one just like that," she said in a

very small voice. "And I know what I'll call it."

"What?"

"Peony."

David had never heard that word before. But he liked the sound of it. "That's a great name," he said. "I'm going to call my cat Peony."

"But I'm going to call *my* cat Peony!" said Paloma.

"So?" said David.

Paloma's funny feeling got funnier. I mean, stronger. She still didn't let the feeling out, even though she was very sure she didn't want David to call his cat Peony. But she was afraid to say so in case the feeling burst out. She backed away from David and closed the front door without even saying goodbye.

Outside the door, David stood frowning. Why had Paloma done that? It wasn't like her. He thought of doing their special ring again, but he decided not to, and began carrying his cat back home.

On the way, he tried out the new name.

"Peony. Peony? Hallo! That's your name – Peony!"

The cat wasn't listening. He was looking around. He liked what he saw. *Openness. Freedom. Adventure!*

So it happened that David very nearly lost his cat on the first day, because, as he turned into his own gate, the cat jumped right out of his arms and made off along the pavement.

David was so shocked he couldn't move at first. But then he saw the cat stop running. He stood for a moment, looking around, his tail waving. This meant he wasn't sure of himself, and somehow David knew this.

David did absolutely the right thing. He didn't chase after him. He walked very quietly to where he was and made a noise like "*shh-wshh-wshh...*" The cat turned his head to look (*Hmmm, interesting noise...*), but he didn't run away. Very slowly and carefully, David got close enough, and picked him up.

The cat thought, *Not yet. I won't run*

away yet. This is all too strange.

So he didn't struggle, and David, feeling relief as sharp as pain, carried him home, stroking and talking to him all the way.

Meanwhile, Paloma managed not to let her feeling out until she was alone in her bedroom. She buried her face in an armful of toy cats and made them damp. But after a bit, she thought, "If David's got a cat, maybe Mummy and Daddy will let me have one."

That made her feel better. She felt sorry now that she hadn't been nicer to David about his cat. "After all," she

thought, "it *is* his birthday." She got up from the bed and went to her table and began to make him a birthday card.

With a cat on it, of course. Paloma was very good at drawing cats. She loved doing the blue eyes.

4. More Badness

When David told his parents he was going to call his cat Peony, his father burst out laughing.

"That's a funny name for a cat!"

"It's a very funny name for *that* cat," said his mother. "It's a boy cat, and Peony is the name of a flower."

That made David stop. But only for a moment. He could be quite stubborn when he'd made up his mind. "He won't know that," he said.

But it seemed as if the cat *did* know he'd been given a really un-boysy name. Because, when David put him down and said, "You like your new name, don't you?" the cat showed what he felt about it by peeing on the floor.

David's mum gave a shriek. "Get that cat out of here!"

David took his cat into the other room and sat him on his knee, stroking him. He seemed to like it best when David did a long, slow stroke from his head to the beginning of his tail, and then gave his tail a very gentle pull.

While he stroked, David thought hard. "Paloma wants to call her cat Peony

when she gets one," he said. "Maybe I'd better change your name," David said. "Would you mind?"

His cat purred loudly. Frankly, he couldn't have cared less.

"Shall I just call you Tom, because you're a tomcat?" David wondered.

But 'Tom' was too ordinary for such a special cat. Carrying his cat over his shoulder, he went to look at his cat book.

He'd already found a picture in it of a cat very like his – white, fluffy, with blue eyes. Now he read what was written under the picture. It said, "A typical Van cat from Turkey."

"Van," said David. "Van? No, I might as well call you Bus or Truck." But then he thought, *Turkey. Turk. Turk!* He liked 'Turk'. He *loved* 'Turk'! You couldn't have a more boysy name than that, and it

wasn't ordinary, either!

"That's it!" he shouted. "Turk! That's your name! Here, Turk, come to me, Turk, Turk!"

Turk – and that's his name from now on – gave his tail a shake, and peed on the carpet, just as David's mum walked in.

"That's it!" she screamed. She picked the cat up by the skin on his neck and carried him through to the garden.

"There," she said. "That's where good cats pee – outside!" And she slammed the back door.

"Mum!" cried David. "You *said* don't let him loose outside before he knows where he lives!"

"He's got to get trained," she said. "I'm not having him peeing in the house. No, David, leave him now, he'll be safe enough in the garden." And she shooed him upstairs to do his homework.

5. From Bad to Worse

Imagine how unwilling David was to leave Turk out there alone!

Turk, however, didn't mind at all. He strolled around exploring, and soon found out how to get over the wall into the next garden. Which was the garden of Paloma's house.

Paloma happened to be looking out through the French window of her kitchen, and saw him.

"Look, Mummy!" she said. "There's David's new cat! I do wish I had a cat. Couldn't I, Mummy, please, please, please?"

"We'll think about it," her mum said. She went out and shooed Turk back over the wall.

Turk started scratching around. He found some nice soft earth where David's dad had been planting new plants. He soon managed to dig them all up in order to make a nice, comfortable loo.

Turk felt very pleased with himself. He rolled around among the scratched-up plants, and got very earthy. Then he started to wash himself, but that was boring, and he didn't like the taste of

earth. So he stopped, and decided he was hungry.

He stalked a beetle, but when he caught it, he thought, *Yuck!* Then he saw a bird on the lawn. It looked to him like a roast chicken would to you. He chased it, but it flew away.

That made him hungrier than ever. He went and stood outside the back door and meowed very loudly. Boy cats are good at that.

David hadn't been doing much homework. Now he belted down the stairs to let his cat in.

"Good cat, you *do* know where you live!" he said. He didn't even notice how dirty the cat was, because who cares about a bit of dirt?

Turk meowed and twined himself round David's legs. It was a lovely feeling. David showed him where his bowls were and put some dry food into one of them. His mum and dad had told him very firmly that it was his job to feed his cat, and this first time was thrilling. He had a cat that peed and ate and went outdoors and came back! A real, live,

living, breathing, eating, peeing cat! He suddenly realised that watching *Aristocats* again and again was *silly.* Even armoured Japanese warrior cats were silly compared to this.

When Turk had cleaned out the bowl, he actually put both front paws up on David's knees. David thought he was saying thank you. Or even, perhaps, *I'm yours and I love you.* He stroked Turk's head and wanted to shout for joy.

(I hate to tell you this, but what Turk was actually saying at this stage was, *Good grub, got any more?* Unfortunately, this person didn't seem to understand simple cat language. The head-stroking was nice, though.)

Turk now made a complete tour of the house. He wanted to pick out his favourite sleeping spot. This turned out to

be at the foot of David's bed, which had a white duvet on it. By the time David came to bed that night, full of birthday cake and carrying presents, he found he had a half-white and half-grey duvet.

Did he care? Not a bit. He was so excited that his cat wanted to sleep with him! But he wasn't stupid. When his mum called up the stairs to see if David wanted her to come and kiss him goodnight, he called back, "No, Mum, don't bother, I'm OK!"

But, of course, she saw the grey duvet in the morning. It was a lot greyer by then.

"That's it!" she said. "I'm making a rule! That Cat is Not Allowed on the Beds!"

Oh, well. Mothers make rules, and cats break them, and that's that. Over the next few days, Turk tried out all the beds in the house and made dents lined with

earth and white hairs in all of them. The more David's mum chased him off, the more he sneaked up and jumped on the beds some more.

In fact, he jumped on chairs, sofas, tables and shelves, any time he felt like it, leaving dirty paw-marks everywhere. Keeping him off the kitchen units became a serious problem. Especially when there was any food about. Turk seemed to think stolen people-food was much nicer than what went into his bowl.

After Turk stole half a chicken while the family was eating the other half in the dining room, David's mother nearly went spare.

"That cat is a bandit!" she cried, and chased Turk outdoors for the night.

Turk did something else too. Something boy cats do. He sprayed. It's not quite the same as peeing, but very like it. The smell is awful, and very hard to get out. One night Turk sprayed David's school-bag. It stank all day at school – even the teacher noticed it and went round scowling and saying, "If anyone thinks that's funny..." Not that David minded. He told everyone to have a sniff – he explained it was the scent his cat put on things to mark his territory.

But at home, David's mum said to his dad, "That cat will have to be Seen To." She meant an operation that makes boy cats stop spraying.

David's dad, who was reading the paper, crossed his legs and said, "All

right, but not just yet." He liked the cat, which was lucky, because David's mum didn't like him at all, and she liked him less and less as the days passed. She was secretly wondering if buying David this cat – which, by the way, was incredibly expensive – had been such a great idea.

6. A Good Wash

One evening a few weeks later, Turk didn't come in when David called him for his dinner.

David was very worried. What if he'd run away, or got lost? But he hadn't. He pretended not to hear David calling. He hid under a bush, until it got dark. Then

he jumped on the wall and started making the most horrendous noises.

Boy cats often do that. They yowl and they growl and they screech. Then other boy cats come and join in. It's like a cat-party, only often they have a fight. That makes even more noise.

David's parents and Paloma's parents couldn't get to sleep because of the awful row Turk and his pals were making.

"Let's not get Paloma a cat, if it's going to make a noise like that!" said Paloma's dad.

"We'll get her a girl cat," said her mum. "Girl cats don't yowl and screech and fight."

Next morning David woke up early. He ran downstairs in his pyjamas and opened the back door. Right away he saw Turk.

But he got a shock. Turk wasn't even grey. He was black – and red. He'd been fighting and rolling in the dirt. One of his ears was bleeding where another cat had chewed it.

David rushed out in his bare feet and picked Turk up in his arms. He didn't care about anything except that his cat was hurt.

"Oh, you poor thing!" he said, stroking him. Turk was tired and hungry and his ear was stinging. Being stroked felt good. *Just what I need*, he thought. David carried him indoors.

When David's mum came downstairs to make breakfast, she was tired and cross from not sleeping. She found David, with dirty feet and dirty pyjamas, sitting on the floor of the kitchen. The fridge door was open. David was feeding Turk bits of raw fish. (*Delicious!* thought Turk,

and nipped David's finger trying to grab a bit more.)

"Just look at that awful cat! He's filthy! Put him down, David!" she said. "And stop feeding him! That fish was for our dinner!" She slammed the fridge door. "Isn't it enough he kept us awake half the night?"

David could tell she was really annoyed. But he didn't put Turk down. He held him tight and ran upstairs with him to the bathroom.

"What you need is a good wash," David said to him. "If you're not clean, Mum will want to get rid of you!"

He shut the door so the cat couldn't get out. Then he ran some warm water into the washbasin. He picked Turk up and tried to dip him into the water to wash him.

It's funny that all those cat books David had read didn't tell him that cats don't like getting wet.

When Turk felt his legs going into the water he let out a cat-shriek and shot into the air. He fell into the bath. There was no water, but Turk jumped out so fast, you'd have thought it had a shark in it.

David tried to catch him. *Let me out of here!* thought Turk, and did another jump – right into the toilet.

Now David made his big mistake. Before Turk could scramble out, David flushed the toilet. He thought that would give his cat a good shower to clean him. Turk let out an ear-splitting yowl. David's mum came running up the stairs.

"What on earth's going on?" she cried, opening the bathroom door.

That was *her* big mistake.

Turk came shooting out like a rocket. He got tangled up in her legs. She lost her balance and landed on the floor. On her behind, which hurt. Turk went streaking down the stairs, hardly touching them, like a – well, like a cataract. He was the wettest cat you ever saw. And the angriest and scaredest.

They're trying to kill me! he thought.

He ran all over the ground floor of the house, leaving wet footprints and drips everywhere. He was trying to find a way out, but there wasn't one. David and his mum found him lying on the sofa shivering and muttering under his breath. There was a big wet puddle on the sofa – a dirty puddle with earth and white hairs in it.

David's mum picked Turk up. She held him out in front of her so as not to get wet. She ran into the kitchen and almost threw him out of the back door. Then she shut it, so he couldn't get back in.

Just at that moment, the front doorbell rang.

It was the neighbour from the other side. She'd come to complain about the cat-party in the night. David heard his mum saying how sorry she was. "I really

don't know what we're going to do about that awful cat," she said.

One of the subtitles on the warrior-cat film was: "Your Doom Is Sealed!"

David and Paloma liked to say it to each other in special doomy voices when one of them was in trouble. It always made them giggle. Now these words went through David's head, and it wasn't a joke. If Turk didn't stop doing bad things, David really thought he wouldn't have his precious cat much longer.

7. A Good Cat Arrives

Turk had to lick himself now, boring or not. He sat on the cold patio and licked and licked. In the end he was a very skinny-looking cat, with all his fur sticking to him.

He didn't feel like staying outside. He was hungry. And where was his food?

Inside the house, of course. He needed to get back in, only he couldn't, because his family hadn't got round to fitting a cat flap yet. But when he hopped over the wall into Paloma's garden, he found the back door of her house open.

He slipped inside.

There was nobody in the kitchen, but Turk could smell there was some food on the table. He jumped right up there. He found a bowl of cereal and milk, and he lost no time in polishing it off to the last delicious drop. But just then he heard someone coming. He jumped down very quickly, and managed to knock the cereal bowl on to the floor.

Crash!

Paloma came running in. She saw Turk streaking out of the back door and over the wall, and saw her cereal bowl on the floor.

Luckily it was plastic and hadn't broken.

She was just going to call for her mother when she had a Thought: *If Mum sees what David's cat did, she won't let me have one.*

She quickly picked up the bowl, and wiped away the paw-marks with a cloth. When her mum came into the kitchen and saw the empty bowl, she said, "Good girl, you ate all your cereal!" (I have to tell you that Paloma was a bit of a fusspot about food.)

Paloma didn't want to tell a lie, so she just went "Mpfff." Then she said, "When are we going to get a *cat,* Mum?"

"Maybe soon," said her mum. "Maybe even today! I've heard of someone who has some kittens for sale."

"Are they white ones?" asked Paloma eagerly.

"I don't know, we'll have to wait and see."

Paloma felt incredibly happy. She ran next door to see David.

"We're going to get my kitten today!" she said, all alight with excitement. "A white one, like yours!"

David didn't seem to be listening.

"I'm really scared," he said. "Mum doesn't like my cat. I think she's going to want to get rid of him."

"What? She can't!" cried Paloma.

"I've got to think how to make her like him."

Paloma thought about it. "Does he sit on her lap?"

"No. He won't. He doesn't sit on laps much."

"Try putting him on her knee. I'm sure she'd get to like stroking him, he's so soft and yummy to touch."

David said he'd try.

8. White Cat? Black Cat!

Paloma's mum and dad took her out in the car that same afternoon. They drove to a house where a strange lady invited them in to look at her kittens.

"They're really adorable," she said. "I hate to part with them. You're going to love them, sweetie, I bet," she added to

Paloma. "You won't know which to choose!"

Paloma was madly excited. She forgot to be shy and ran to the deep basket where the kittens were. She was so sure that they'd be white that when she peeped in and they weren't, she couldn't believe it.

"But they're black!" she almost shouted. "And they're not fluffy!"

She was so disappointed she plonked herself down on the floor and burst into tears. Her mum stooped beside her and put her arms around her.

"Don't you want one, then?"

"No! No! I wanted a white fluffy one like David's!"

She was crying so loudly, it sounded a bit like the noise boy cats make when they're having a night party. (She was caterwauling.)

Her dad didn't say a word. He picked one little black kitten out of the basket and put it into Paloma's hands.

It was the smoothest, softest, warmest thing she'd ever touched. And the most alive.

She forgot to cry. She began to stroke the little thing. It stood up on her leg and stretched itself. It had a pointed face, pointed ears and a little pointed tail.

When it finished stretching and yawning, it opened its eyes. They weren't blue. They were green. It looked straight at her, and meowed. A high kitten-meow.

Paloma had spent so many hours playing with her toy cats, and talking cats with David, that she could understand cat-language. She knew this kitten was saying, "I want to belong to you."

She sat there on the floor, stroking it. She forgot about wanting a fluffy white cat. Her tears dried on her cheeks. This little black thing was her cat and she wanted no other.

"This one," she said softly. "This one."

9. The Second Peony

Luckily the one she'd chosen was a girl cat. I mean, kitten. Paloma immediately announced that her name was Peony.

"But isn't that what David calls his cat?" asked her mum.

"I don't care. It was my name that I

thought of. I can't help it if David—"

She didn't want to say 'stole it'. David was her friend and stealing, even a name, was bad. But she wasn't going to *not* call her cat Peony just because David had called his cat that first.

"Won't it be confusing?" her mum asked.

Paloma said, "Oh, he's changed his cat's name! His is called Turk. Didn't I tell you?"

They stopped at the shops on the way home. They bought two bowls, and a post with rope wrapped round it. That was so Peony could scratch and sharpen her claws. They bought a litter-tray and a bag of litter, which was to make a loo for the kitten, and of course they bought lots of kitten food.

"I'll cope with the litter-tray, but it'll

be your job to feed her," her mum said.

Paloma said, "Of course. I'll never forget. She's my cat and I'll be—" She stopped.

"Cat-sponsible?" joked her mum.

"That's not a proper cat word, but I will be, I promise," said Paloma seriously, though inside she was laughing with happiness.

When they got home and had arranged everything, the next thing Paloma did was to put the kitten back in its carry-box and take it next door to show David.

She did their special ring. When David came to the door, Paloma saw at once that he looked miserable.

"What's up?" she asked. "Has there been a cat-astrophe?"

"Well, a bit," he said. "I did your idea. I

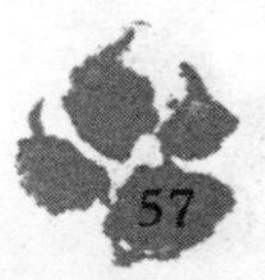

put Peony on Mum's lap for a surprise. He... he sprayed her."

"Oh! Well, maybe you could tell her that's cat-language for 'I love you'."

"I did," said David with a shudder. (His mum had said, "Is that so? Well, please tell me in cat-language how to say, 'If you do that again, I'll wring your neck!'")

Paloma didn't realise how bad this was. She was too excited to worry about David's problem. "Look what I've got!"

She put the carry-box on the doorstep and took off the lid. David crouched down and stroked the kitten.

"He's a bit of black magic," he said.

"He's a she," said Paloma.

"It's so great now we both have cats," he said. "What are you going to call her?"

"Peony, of course!"

"Well, that's OK. Good that I changed mine."

"Yes!" she said happily, then added quickly, "Turk's a much better name for a boy cat anyway."

Just at that moment, Turk came strolling down the passage to the front door. He'd smelled another cat in his territory.

He walked to the carry-box and put his head in. The new kitten shrank down inside.

"She's scared," said David. He picked up Turk. Paloma picked up Peony. They brought the two cats' noses together. The kitten put out her little tongue and licked the big white cat's pink nose.

David's bad cat growled. He put up his paw with all the claws out.

"Oh, look," said David. "You see, he's got protractible claws. That means he can stick them out." That was

information straight out of his favourite cat-book.

"Pro-nothing! He's being nasty!" Paloma said, backing away.

David was embarrassed. It was true. He backed away too. "I'm sorry," he said.

"Never mind," said Paloma. "They'll get to like each other. They'll have to. They're going to be neighbours."

David thought she was being very nice about it. But when she'd gone, he told his cat off. "You mustn't be nasty to Paloma's kitten!"

Turk took absolutely no notice. He was thinking, *If that other cat comes anywhere near my territory, I'll...* Well. He didn't know what he'd do. But it would be something *really* bad.

10. Turk Does Himself No Good

Paloma's kitten grew up fast. She wasn't a bad cat like Turk. She was probably as good as any cat ever is.

She soon learnt to use her litter-box. She was very dainty and careful and didn't knock things over. When Paloma tied a cotton mouse to a piece of string

and the string to a garden cane, and pretended to fish for the kitten, she jumped up to grab the bait just like a trout out of a stream. Paloma couldn't understand why she'd wanted a fluffy white cat. More and more as she grew, Peony looked like Slinky Malinki.

Paloma's days were changed. She played with the kitten before school, and put her food down for her, and all day she looked forward to getting home and finding Peony there waiting, ready to play and be loved. When Paloma stroked her, she purred like a motorbike engine.

The sound of Peony's purring made Paloma feel all warm inside. It seemed so easy to make her happy. All you had to do was feed her and love her and she was happy and good.

Well... she did have one bad habit. She stole Paloma's toy cats. She would creep up to Paloma's bedroom and pick up a toy in her teeth and carry it off to one of her favourite places in the house, and play with it. At first Paloma got in a panic when a toy was missing, but she soon learnt where to look. She thought it was funny, Peony stealing toys for herself. She only minded when Peony took them into the garden and they got rained on.

Her mum, like David's, made rules. Peony wasn't allowed on the beds, or the table. Unlike Turk, Peony didn't break the rules. Her favourite place was on the back of one of the big armchairs in the living-room.

Paloma boasted to David about how good Peony was. But she still liked to

hear what terrible things Turk had got up to.

One day Turk came into the house, through the new catflap, carrying something in his mouth. Something limp and smelly. He carried it carefully to where David's mum was sitting in the kitchen, quietly drinking a cup of tea, and laid it across her feet.

She looked down. There on her best shoes lay a dead rat. Turk was looking up at her through his blue, innocent eyes.

Well, of course, she let out a scream, and leapt up so suddenly that the cup and saucer went flying, and so did the tea. So did the rat. "Ugh! Oh, you disgusting cat, it's horrible, take it out!"

David came running. He found her shaking her skirt, which was all wet with

tea. The saucer was broken. The rat lay on the floor. Turk was crouched over it. He picked it up and looked as if he were offering it to her.

"Get it out! Get it out!" she kept shouting.

"Mum – please – you don't understand – it's a present!"

"A *what?!*"

"Yes! It says in the cat book! When they bring you something they've caught, it means they love you!"

"That cat," said his mother between her teeth, "doesn't love anybody. And don't ask me how *I* feel about *him*! Now take that hateful thing away!"

"Mum! Turk's not hateful!"

"The *rat*, I meant!"

(But I'm not so sure she did mean the rat. And neither was David.)

David picked it up by the tail and carried it out into the garden, where he dug a hole and buried it. Turk followed him. David stroked him.

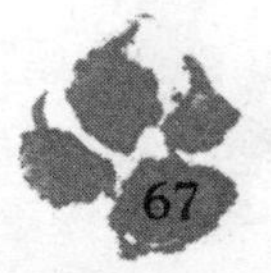

"She didn't mean to hurt your feelings," he said. "But don't do it again. And don't try it with a bird, either." He shuddered. If it had been a bird…! His mum loved birds. That would've been the end, for sure!

Suddenly his mum burst out of the house. Turk turned tail and fled. He knew danger when he saw it – she was after him! He even had a sort of idea what he'd done wrong.

"He's done it again!" she shouted. "He's sprayed in the living room, I can smell it! That's IT! He'll have to be Seen To or – or – he'll just have to *go*!"

David rushed up to her.

"No, Mum, no! Please don't say that! He's a lovely cat, he doesn't mean to be bad! All he needs is to – to grow up a bit, he's only a baby…"

"A baby? That – that polar bear? If he grows any more we'll have to get the doors made bigger!"

"I'll train him, Mum. I'll teach him. Please don't be angry with him!"

David's mum looked into his pleading eyes.

"All right, David," she said. "I'm sorry. Sometimes things get too much. I think I need a holiday."

She went indoors, leaving David feeling helpless and scared. It was all very well to talk about 'training' Turk, but how do you train a bad cat to be good?

11. The Night Party

Paloma's dad finally got round to buying a catflap and fitting it into the back door. Paloma held Peony and gently pushed her through the catflap until she got the idea. Till now she had always been shut in at night and only allowed out in the daytime. Now she

could come and go as she liked.

On her first night outside, she met Turk for the second time.

This didn't go too well.

She walked happily around her garden, sniffing all the different smells (so much sharper at night, somehow), and eating some lovely grass. Suddenly a white something dropped as if from nowhere right in front of her.

It was Turk, of course. By this point he'd decided Paloma's garden was part of his territory, no matter how often Paloma's mum and dad shooed him out. Peony started away, but then walked up to him and tried to touch noses.

"Hsssssss!" hissed Turk. "Get away from me, you skinny little black toe-claw!"

Peony sat down and washed her face.

"Are all fat white cats as rude as you?" she asked.

"How dare you say I'm fat! Fluffy isn't fat! Get out of my territory before I scratch your ear off!"

"Like somebody nearly did to yours?" asked Peony sweetly. "That must hurt a lot. Let me lick it better for you."

And she tried to. He backed away. Let

some little girl cat lick his ear? Not likely! "Keep off! I'm the Big Cat around here, and don't you forget it!"

"Maybe in your own territory. This is my garden."

"It's part of my range. I've sprayed all over it."

"Yes, I noticed," she said. "But it's still my garden. "

"I suppose you're going to chase me out of it!"

"No. I don't mind you being here, if you don't hiss at me."

Turk was baffled. He sat down a little way away and stared at her.

"I've never been out at night before," Peony said. "What shall we do?"

"I'm going to call a night party," said Turk. "But girl cats can't come."

"Oh? Why not?"

"Because night parties are strictly for boy cats."

"All right," she said. "I'll just stay and watch."

"It'll be on the wall," he said. "Of course, you're too small to climb up there."

This was true. She was only just fully grown and she hadn't done much climbing. But she saw there was a tree that leaned up against the wall. She'd been climbing her scratching post since she was a kitten. A scratching post was very like a tree.

She *protracted* her claws and got a good grip on the tree. After the first little bit, it got easier, and soon she had hiked herself up to the top of the wall. She'd never been so high up before. It was great up here. She could see all the

gardens around and smell lots of different smells.

Suddenly she smelled one that made her stiffen.

"What's that smell?" she asked.

"Dog," said Turk. "There's a rotten dog that lives over there."

"Why is he rotten?"

"*Why is he rotten?* Are you stupid? Because he's a dog, that's why!"

Peony was more sure than ever that this cat was the rudest cat it was possible to live next door to. She thought of jumping down and going home, but she didn't.

Turk started making yowling noises. Soon some other boy cats arrived. They sat along the wall and made even louder noises than Turk. It seemed as if each one was trying to make more noise than the others.

Peony yawned.

After a bit, one of the boy cats pounced on another and began hissing and scratching and biting. It was really scary for Peony. She moved closer to Turk.

"Is this the night party?" she asked. "If so, I don't think I like it much."

"Rubbish! This is fun!" said Turk between yowls. But still, he sat on the

wall between Peony and the two cats who were fighting. At last they fought so hard, they fell right off the wall. They landed in the flowerbed and shot off in different directions.

Peony stood up. “I think night parties are silly,” she said. “I’m going home.”

“Go on then!” said Turk.

She didn’t know him well enough to see that really he wished she’d stay.

She decided not to go down by the tree, like a kitten. She wasn't a kitten any more. So she pointed her head at the ground, on her side of the wall, and slithered down to the bottom, gripping with her claws. She didn't land very well and clinging to the bricks made her claws hurt, but she'd done it and she felt good about that.

She slipped through the catflap and had a snack. Then she went and sat in her favourite place on the back of the armchair. She gave herself a good wash and then went to sleep, thinking, "Boy cats are stupid. I'm so glad I'm a girl cat."

Outside the cats were still yowling. But after a while they all went home. All except Turk.

12. A Brave Little Cat

Turk jumped down from the wall and pushed his way through Peony's catflap.

In her sleep, Peony heard it go 'clack'. She woke up at once and lifted her head, her ears pricked forward. She listened for a moment, then jumped to the floor and ran into the kitchen.

Turk was sniffing one of her bowls.

"Is this what they give you to eat?" he said. "Smells good."

And he began to eat Peony's food! She didn't like that one bit. In fact she couldn't believe it.

"You should go away," she said. "This is my house."

Turk finished the food and licked his lips. "I like it here. I think I'll stick around," he said.

Something new and strange was happening inside Peony. She was not happy about this. She knew Turk shouldn't be here. And what was this faint growling sound she was making?

Turk went into the living room. Peony went after him, her tail sticking straight up and the fur on her shoulders starting to bristle. Turk was clawing the armchair.

"What are you doing?" she asked.

"Sharpening my claws. What does it look like?"

"I have a special place for that," said Peony. "I never sharpen my claws on their things."

"I do. All the time." And he did some more of it.

"You should go home!" said Peony. That was definitely a growl. It surprised her.

He looked at her. "And if I don't – you're going to *do* something to me?" he asked. "A skinny little black girl cat like you? I don't think so."

And to make his point, he actually sprayed the leg of the armchair.

The strange feeling Peony had was getting stronger. This was her house. This big white boy cat shouldn't be here,

eating her food and spoiling things.

Now he was up on the back of the armchair. He was curling up – in her favourite place!

She put her ears back, opened her mouth, and hissed. She'd never hissed before. She'd never been so angry before.

"Go away – now!" she spat furiously.

He peered down at her, his white face like a – well, I was going to compare it to the moon on a dark night, but to Peony it just looked like what it was – the face of a big white boy cat that shouldn't be there.

"You can't make me go! Just you try!" he hissed.

That did it.

Peony made a mighty leap, and landed on him. They were suddenly a tangled ball of legs and ears and teeth and fur – black fur and white fur, mixed. They fell off the chair with a thump, with Turk on top. Peony felt a pain where she'd landed on the floor. That made her really lose it.

Turk had had fights – plenty of them. But never like this. They bounced from the floor to the sofa and from the sofa to the floor. Turk jumped on the table. Peony jumped on top of him. They knocked a lot of things on to the floor, making a terrific noise.

Peony was as fierce as a little black panther. She was biting and scratching – hissing and snarling. At last, Turk couldn't take it any more.

He broke away, and fled through the catflap, leaving it going *clack-clack-clack* behind him.

The noise of the fight had woken Paloma and her mum and dad. They came running down the stairs. They found their good little Peony looking like a witch's cat, her tail like a bottle-brush, her back arched and her mouth like a

snake, still hissing.

The room was a mess. There was white fur all over the place. It was even in the air, as if a pillow had burst.

"Peony! What happened? Are you all right?" cried Paloma. She picked her up and stroked all her black fur smooth again. She held her to her face and kissed her – something her mum said was unhygienic. But this time she didn't say anything.

"She was guarding the house," said Paloma's dad. "What a brave little cat! Looks like she sent that bad cat from next door packing!"

They made a big fuss of Peony. They filled up her food bowl from a nice fresh sachet of Felix. Rules were forgotten. Peony slept on Paloma's bed that night.

Turk crept home through the dark. He

felt awful. He was scratched and bitten. He was stinging all over. But that wasn't the worst. His pride was hurt. A little girl cat had made him run away.

He crept up to David's room and slithered on to the bed. He licked his scratches and bites for a long time. Then he slid under the duvet.

He wanted to hide himself. He curled up next to David's feet. When he fell asleep, he had horrible cat-dreams. He dreamed of being on the wall. A lot of his boy cat friends came and cat-laughed at him. They knew. They'd seen. He felt ashamed. Not ashamed of being bad – of course not. Ashamed of being beaten by a girl cat.

He woke up thinking he'd never dare to show his whiskers outdoors again.

13. David and Paloma Have a Row

The day after the big fight, Paloma's mum went to talk to David's mum. They had a coffee together. Did they have a lovely motherly gossip? Of course not. They talked cats.

"Your cat got into our house last night," Paloma's mum said.

David's mum passed the biscuits. "I'm not at all surprised! That cat's into everything! What happened? Did your cat have a fight with him?"

"Yes, she did. And she beat him too."

"He's in a real mess. He won't go out now. He just creeps under the sofa and makes muttering noises. David says that's how cats swear! Poor David's very upset. I can't bear the cat, myself, but David loves him. I don't know what to do."

They had another biscuit and talked about litter-trays. The litter-trays in both houses were being used again, because Peony wouldn't go out, either.

After a while, David's mum started to talk about summer holidays. She said they were going to Wales to stay in a cottage. The cottage had room for another family. She asked if Paloma's

family might like to come too.

"The children would love it. It's right by the sea, and they could play together."

Paloma's mum thought this was a pretty good idea. She said she'd talk to Paloma's dad about it. Neither of the mothers thought for a moment that their kids wouldn't want to go if it meant leaving the cats behind.

And it did mean that. The cottage was a no-pets zone. The owners were allergic to all animals. Especially cats.

While the holiday business was being settled by the grown-ups, Paloma's mum invited David for a play-date with Paloma. Paloma liked David and all that, but a play-date? Play-dates were with other girls. Besides, she wasn't feeling like talking cats with David. Not after what had happened.

The minute they were left alone, she said, “Turk shouldn’t have come into our house.”

“Peony shouldn’t have bitten and scratched him.”

“Turk’s a burglar.”

“Peony’s cruel.”

“She is not cruel! She was guarding the house!”

"Turk was just visiting, like I visit you! What would happen if you started biting and scratching *me?*"

"Well, I might, if you came in the night without being asked!"

David thought this was an awful thing to say.

"I'm glad I've got a tom! Toms are much better than queens!" David was showing off by using the right words for male and female cats, but things were getting out of hand.

The next thing would have been, "Boys are better than girls!" and "Girls are better than boys!" But before they could get into that, Paloma's mum suggested going out for a pizza, so the rowing had to stop. But it wasn't much of a play-date. They ended up (despite the pizzas) not speaking to each other.

"This is too silly," Paloma's mum scolded, when she found out about it. "Well, you'll have to get over it, because we're all going on holiday together."

"With the cats," said Paloma. It wasn't a question. It was an of-course-we'll-take-them. But her mum said, "I'm afraid not."

Paloma stared at her. "We're *not* taking them?" Her mum shook her head. "But – but – but – what'll happen to them? We can't just leave them here alone!"

"No, of course not. We're putting them in a cattery."

This was one cat word Paloma hadn't heard. "A what-ery?"

"It's a special place where cats can be looked after while their families go away."

"Will she be in a cage?"

"Er – well... she might."

"You mean – a cat prison?"

"No, no! It's – it's just a nice friendly place. She'll be perfectly happy there."

"Without us? In a strange place? In a *cage*? She'll hate it!"

"Of course she won't! Anyway, she'll have to go. We can't take her with us."

Paloma forgot all about not speaking to David. She was round at his house in a flash. She rang their special ring. David came slowly. He was still not speaking.

"I've got a new cat-word," said Paloma grimly. "'Cat-tery.' It's a prison for cats."

David scowled. "What do you mean?"

"We're supposed to be going on holiday together, you and us, and the grown-ups are putting our cats in some horrible place while we're away!"

After a moment, David said, "Well, I'm not going."

"Me neither! I won't go without Peony!"

Their row forgotten, they did spit-in-your-hand-and-do-high-fives. That was their way of promising. Unless they could take the cats, they wouldn't go anywhere. And nobody could make them.

Well, of course that turned out to be just empty words. Because, when grown-ups say something is going to happen, the kids can make all the fuss they like. It's going to happen.

14. Peony and Turk Make it Up

A few days went by. Turk and Peony began to feel a bit better after their fight. They missed going out. One night Peony felt brave. She pushed her way out through the catflap. Not her usual little jump – she went leg by leg, looking all around.

She was still feeling upset. She knew girl

cats aren't meant to fight.

Outside in the cat-friendly darkness, she felt like her old self. She climbed the tree on to the wall and sat quietly, looking down into the next garden. The moon came out from behind a cloud. Suddenly she saw the catflap next door open and a white head poked slowly out.

Turk had had a cat-to-cat talk to himself. *If I don't go out*, he thought, *they'll think I'm scared. Maybe that – that – that – girl cat thing hasn't told anyone she beat me.*

Anyway, he was bored to death staying indoors all the time.

Peony crouched down into the ivy. It hid her completely.

Turk slithered through his catflap. He looked around. He couldn't see any other cats. He walked carefully to the wall, and took a flying leap.

He landed – right on top of Peony.
He got an awful fright. She did too.

After a brief skirmish, they both fell off the wall on opposite sides. They didn't go back through their catflaps. They just crouched there. Turk was on the moonlit side. He looked like a ghost cat. Peony was on the dark side. She looked like a shadow.

At last, Turk made a soft sound. Peony heard it. He said, "I didn't see you."

She said, "It didn't hurt." She wanted to say, "I'm sorry I bit you." But she decided not to. She thought he might not want to think about that any more. And she was quite right. What he wanted was to forget all about it.

But he wasn't ready to do anything that might look as if he wasn't still the local Big Cat.

"Come back on the wall," he said in a bossy, Big Cat sort of way.

She climbed the tree on to the wall.

"What are you doing out here?" Turk asked her.

"I came out to... to see if you'd come out," she said.

"Of course I came out! Why wouldn't I?" He wondered if she'd come out every

night since the fight, looking for him.

"Well, that's all right then," she said.

They sat there in the moonlight, looking at each other. Turk knew their fight was over. He was glad, suddenly. Very glad. In fact, he felt gladder than he'd ever felt before.

Peony saw that Turk had a big, raw scratch on his nose.

She put her head forward slowly. That brought her nose close to his. He didn't move away or say anything. She put out her tongue and licked him.

He sat very still and closed his eyes. She moved a little way away. He moved after her.

In David's house, the moonlight shone on his face and woke him up. He loved moonlight. He got out of bed and went to the window. Against the full moon, he saw

a silhouette: two cats, side by side, very close together.

He leaned out of the window and stared at them. Tomorrow the cats were to

be taken to the cattery. Everything he and Paloma could think of to stop it, they had done. In their separate houses, they'd begged. They'd pleaded. They'd even said they didn't want to go on holiday! But it hadn't changed a thing.

David suggested that instead of putting Turk in a cattery, they leave lots of food for him. "Enough for two weeks?" said his dad. "I don't think so! Besides, we have to lock the catflap so no strays will get in."

Next door, Paloma caterwauled. "Peony will be miserable!"

"No, she won't. She'll be with other cats. Cats aren't like dogs. She won't miss us."

"Yes, she will! Peony loves me!" Then she thought of something worse. "Maybe she'll forget us, and not know us when we get back!"

Her mum tried to comfort her. She wished she hadn't said about Peony not missing them. She took it back. "She will miss us, but she won't be unhappy. I promise. And she will know us when we come back."

Paloma stopped caterwauling and tried sulking, but nothing helped. They were going to Wales, the cats were going to cat prison, and that was the end of that.

David stood at the window in the moonlight. He thought of the locked catflaps and knew that the cattery was the only answer. He crept back to bed. But he didn't sleep for a long time, and not just because of the moonlight. And it wasn't because he was excited about the holiday, either.

15. Parents With a Problem

Next day the parents in both families woke up early. Their idea was to get the cats into their carry-boxes and to the cattery before the children were awake. And that might have saved some tears, except for one thing.

Neither of the cats had come home.

On each side of the wall, two mums stood calling. But they didn't want to call loudly because they didn't want to wake the children.

"Turk! Turk! Breakfast!" called David's mum in a loud whisper.

"Peony! Oh, Peony! Come on, P., where are you?" hissed Paloma's mum next door.

They *shhh-a-wshh*ed as loudly as they dared. Nothing. After a while Paloma's

mum called over to David's.

"Where can they have gone?"

"Heaven knows! What *are* we going to do?"

"Maybe we should tell the kids that we've put them in the cattery."

"We certainly can't let them think they've run away. They'd be so upset."

Meanwhile the fathers met in the street in front of the houses. They were two very worried men.

"We could leave the catflaps open."

"I really don't want to do that. Two weeks! We could have every cat in the neighbourhood turning our house upside down!"

"What if we ask our neighbours to feed them if they turn up?"

"I'm sure they'll be delighted," said David's dad sarcastically. (There'd been more complaints about the night parties.)

"But we'll have to."

The two dads stood in the street, looking at each other.

"So. We tell the kids a lie – that the cats are safe in the cattery. Is that it?"

"I suppose so. It's awful, but I don't see any other way."

They each went to speak to their neighbours on the other sides of their houses. Neither of the neighbours was at

all pleased. The complaining neighbour, next to David's house, flatly refused.

"People who own cats have to be responsible for them," she said. "I'm sorry, that's a no."

The neighbour next door to Paloma's house was a little bit nicer.

"Oh, all right, if I see them I'll put something out. Will you leave me some food?"

Paloma's dad rushed back into the house and took two big bags of dry food and two bowls to the neighbour. He just got back in time, because Paloma came downstairs and caught him coming in the front door.

"Where've you been, Daddy?"

"I – er... well. To, er... take Peony to the cattery."

"I didn't say goodbye to her!"

Her mum hurried to her side. "Now, Paloma, don't make a fuss, there's a good girl. We're leaving in an hour. Please go up and decide what toys and books you want to take."

Through a rainbow of tears, Paloma noticed something. "Why are you so red in the face, Daddy?"

Her dad hurried away without answering.

Next door, David's dad was telling him the same lie. (I'm really sorry if you thought that parents never tell lies to their children. But you do see that they were in a very difficult situation?)

David also had to decide which special things to bring. At the last minute, when the two families were loading up their cars, he thought of something they'd forgotten – the blow-up rubber dinghy. It had been stored in the garden shed since last summer.

He rushed out to get it. When he came back, his dad was just fastening the catflap shut. David watched. He was feeling very uneasy, without quite knowing why. His dad hadn't looked at him properly all morning.

"Dad. Why is Turk's carry-box in the shed? How did you take him?"

"What? Oh. Well. We used it, of course, and then I put it back."

"It's all dusty, though."

"Yes. I noticed that. Now, hurry up, David, we're ready to leave. Here, I'll help you with the dinghy."

Off they went, in two cars laden with luggage. The two children travelled together in the back of David's family car. David's parents in the front didn't look at each other. (They were feeling *terrible.* As you'd expect.)

Paloma and David talked about how the cats would be feeling in the cattery. David told Paloma what he'd seen in the night, how Turk and Peony had made up their fight.

Would they see each other in the

cattery? They both hoped they would. Or they'd be so lonely.

16. Abandoned

Well, they didn't need to worry about *that.*

Turk and Peony weren't a bit lonely. They'd been together all night, prowling around the moonlit gardens, over walls and under fences and up trees and on to the roofs of sheds, having a whale of a

time. Especially Peony, who'd never had a night adventure before.

They didn't call a night party. They were happy just to have each other.

Turk showed Peony how to hunt. They crouched under some bushes until a mouse ran by. Turk leaped out and pounced. He played with the poor thing for a bit, batting it with his paws. (Sorry, but that's what cats do.) Soon Peony got the idea, and the next mouse that ran by, she had a go. She didn't manage to catch it, but that was because she wasn't trying very hard.

Turk offered her his mouse. She drew back. She'd never tried to eat anything alive before. "No, thank you," she said. "I'm not hungry." Nor was he, so after a bit he let the mouse go.

I'm afraid this was not going to

happen again. Letting the mouse go, I mean. You only play with your food when you're not hungry. When you are, you eat up, quick. Actually, neither of the cats had ever *been* very hungry, because their food was always there in their bowls on the kitchen floor.

When morning came, Peony wanted to go home, but they were rather far away by now and Turk was having fun jumping from one shed roof to the next. But when they finally did find their way home, they got a very nasty surprise. The catflaps on both houses were firmly shut. So were the doors and windows. And the cats knew, right away, that the houses were empty of people.

This gave them both a bad feeling. They each tried meowing loudly outside their back doors, but of course nobody

came. The nicer neighbour next door to Peony's house heard Peony meowing and called her.

"Peony! Come! Get some food!"

But Peony didn't go. She didn't know that voice, even when it said her name. Instead she climbed on to the wall on Turk's side. She could see him prowling about. He jumped on to the kitchen windowsill, and then jumped down again. After a moment he joined her on the wall.

"Can't get in," he said.

"Me neither," she answered. "What shall we do?"

"Don't ask me."

She pushed her head against his. They lay on the wall together for a long time. Turk began thinking about that mouse he'd let go. After a while, he said, "Let's catch something."

"What?"

"A bird?"

"I like birds," she said. "I like watching them."

"Never mind watching them," said Turk. "I want to eat one."

David's mother liked birds too. She had a bird-table, which was supposed to be cat-proof – nice and high so Turk couldn't get on it (so she thought). And until now he never had, because he'd never

needed to. Now he sat on the wall watching birds coming and going to the bird-table, which had some stale bread on it. He was a good jumper. He crouched in the ivy, his hips wiggling. Could he make it, from the wall? No.

He jumped down and went and stood under the bird-table, staring up.

The birds flew away. But when he didn't move, they came back. He listened to them, chirping away happily above his head. Maddening! He couldn't stand it.

With all his claws protracted, he made a scrambling leap up the post and got his front paws over the edge of the table. He hauled himself up. There he stood proudly on the cat-proof bird-table. All by himself, of course. Not a bird in sight.

From the wall, Peony watched him. Somehow she'd known it would be no good. She got down, and hid in a bush. Her tummy was feeling very strange, and this strange feeling made her sure that she could catch a bird if she tried.

I'm sure a lot of you love birds. I love them too. So I won't describe what happened next. But what Peony

discovered was that the strange empty feeling inside made her move much more quickly than ever before. It made her able to do things she hadn't known she could do. And soon her tummy was full again. The strange feeling went away and she sat on the wall watching the birds in a different way than before.

What about Turk? He'd seen what had happened. This girl cat had shown him up again. She had done what he hadn't. She looked happy and full. He felt unhappy and empty.

But somehow this didn't make him angry, like before. He felt sort of proud. As if he'd done the clever thing himself.

This is how they passed their first day without families, while David and Paloma got further and further away, thinking their beloved cats were shut in

a cattery. They didn't feel good about that, but they'd have felt a whole lot worse if they'd known what was really happening.

17. Going Feral

When family cats lose their families, they don't sit around and mope, or pine and die of hunger. They go back to nature. They become *feral*, which means they learn to look after themselves.

But Turk and Peony didn't go back to nature straight away. First they learnt to

be burglars. This was Turk's idea, of course.

There were lots of cats in the neighbourhood, and lots of catflaps, and before two or three days had passed, Turk had found them all. Some of them had special fastenings so that only the right cat could get in, but many of them you just had to push your head against, and there you were, in a strange kitchen, often with food laid out all ready to be stolen.

Peony didn't like doing this sort of thing, but Turk said, "We have to." So she let him go first and then if he meowed for her, she would follow.

But they had to stop these raids, because word went around among the other cats and then there was bad trouble. The cats that the catflaps

belonged to lay in wait for them. Turk would get halfway through a flap and suddenly there would be a hiss and a yowl, and a furry, furious figure would leap at him, and he'd have to back out very fast before he got his head bitten off. (Well, not off exactly, but you know what I mean.)

Backing out of catflaps isn't nearly as easy as going in front-wards. The first time it happened, Turk tried to turn around while he was *in* the catflap. He got stuck, and the cat behind him bit him hard in the ribs. Another time he nearly got his tail bitten off. (Not quite.)

The next time, the owner of the catflap ambushed him before he'd even got to the catflap.

"Aha! There you are, you grub-snatcher! Gotcha!" it yowled.

Turk, caught off-guard, tried to run, but the other cat – a big tom who was supposed to be one of his night party pals – jumped on him and there was a snarling, howling fight. Turk won, but he was beginning to look as if he'd been in a cat war. He was a walking cat-astrophe. Peony licked and licked to make his bites and scratches not hurt so much.

After a couple of bad experiences like that, they kept away from houses. They learned to be good hunters. But soon the birds, mice, rats and squirrels passed the word around that there were two feral cats hunting in the gardens and they kept away, or kept hidden.

Thin times followed. Beetles. Worms. Frogs. Don't ask.

After a lot of days, there came an evening when everybody put their rubbish bags out for the dustbin men to collect the next morning. Prowling about the pavements, his tummy one big hole of hunger, Turk could smell good food. Not the nice food in sachets and bags that he was used to, and not fresh meat. Bones. Leftovers. They were shut up in black sacks, but he could smell them just the same.

There is nothing so good for ripping open plastic sacks as some well-protracted cats' claws. Soon the pavements were scattered with the rubbish that Turk and Peony had dragged out of the torn-open bags.

They went to bed full of junk food that night. Lovely things they'd never eaten before, like Kentucky Fried Chicken. Chicken bones are supposed to be bad for cats. But Peony and Turk didn't know that you could get bone-splinters stuck in your throat. They chewed happily on the bones like a pair of little hyenas.

Did I mention 'bed'? No comfortable armchairs or duvets or (Turk's favourite) the warm place under the radiator for them! They slept curled up together on the ground under a shed. At least it was dry, which was good, because it rained in

the night, and when they woke up, all the smells had changed and the ground was wet. It was still raining. But they had to crawl out just the same because they were hungry again.

It was very early – just getting light. The birds were singing, but high up in the trees, where they couldn't be caught. Turk and Peony crept through a side alley, under a gate, and into the street where the bags were. There were lots of bags they hadn't explored. They found one that smelled good, and they were just going to tear it open when—

"Run!" hissed Turk. "Run hard!"

He was off and gone before Peony could turn around. But when she did, she got such a shock she couldn't run. She just crouched down, every hair of her fur on end and her mouth open wide.

There in front of her was a red animal with long legs and a bushy tail and a pointed nose. He was trying to bite one of the black bags open. But when he saw her, he left the bag. He put his head down low and moved towards her. His lips curled back from his teeth. Those teeth! This animal was hunting.

Have you guessed what it was? It was a fox. An urban fox – that is, one that's come in from the country because of all the food there is in town; easy food that they don't have to catch and kill. But that doesn't mean they're not quite ready to kill, if they see something tasty. Like a little black cat, for instance.

Peony backed away, hissing fiercely. The fox crept after her. She found herself backed against a low wall in front of a house. Did she dare turn and jump over it to get away? She was afraid to take her eyes off this monster.

Suddenly, Turk was there! He was on the wall above her. He didn't wait a moment. He leapt straight at the fox with all his claws out, his mouth snarling, his ears laid flat, his sharp little teeth ready to bite.

When she saw that, Peony stopped being scared. She flew at the fox too. Two of them were too much for that city hunter and he turned and ran, his bushy tail between his back legs. Yelping!

Turk stood for a moment, back arched, fur on end, watching him go.

"That'll teach him to hunt cats!" he said. "We showed him cats are better than dogs!"

"Was that a dog?" asked Peony, rubbing herself along his side to flatten her fur.

"Sort of, I think," Turk said. "Rotten, anyway."

They went back to the bags. But they didn't get anything, because along came the council trucks to take all the bags away. And weren't the men annoyed when they saw the mess – all that rubbish strewn all over the pavement!

"Rotten cats," they told each other.

Which just goes to show it all depends on your point of view, who's rotten and who isn't.

Anyway, by then the two cats had vanished. Back into their wild, dangerous life without families.

18. The Lie is Discovered

Meanwhile, in Wales, things were only *sort of* going well.

First of all there was the weather. There's a lot of weather in Wales. But they could have got around that. You don't have to be on the beach all the time. There's lots to do in Wales and the

children's parents were determined not to let the weather spoil things.

They went to a circus, set up on the fields outside their village. They visited a place where there was an aqueduct, which is like a high bridge across a valley, but instead of a road, it has a canal in it so that boats can go across. The boats are narrow (the canal is only a few feet wide) and the families enjoyed riding the boat and looking over the edge at the river far, far below.

They ate out in all sorts of pubs and cafés and did some shopping (there are lovely things to buy in Wales). They went driving in the mountains. The fathers did a bit of kayaking. It should have been a lovely holiday.

But David and Paloma couldn't completely enjoy themselves. They

couldn't help worrying about their cats.

"Are they missing us? Are they being looked after properly? Have you phoned the cattery to see if they're all right?"

They asked questions until the grown-ups were ready to scream. Especially with what they had on their consciences – you can imagine.

One night in the cottage the children couldn't sleep. The grown-ups were downstairs, talking. There was something about the *way* they were talking that made the children want to listen.

They crept to the top of the narrow stairs and crouched down. The cottage was small and the stairs led straight into the tiny living room.

"I'm sure they'll be all right," David's dad was saying. "They're not like dogs,

after all. They know how to take care of themselves."

"What do?" Paloma whispered to David.

"Shh! Listen!"

"But what if they wander off and don't come back? What'll we tell them then?"

"They'll never forgive us if that happens," said Paloma's mum.

"Who won't? What are they talking about?" whispered Paloma.

David stood up slowly. He walked down the stairs.

All the grown-ups' heads turned at once. You never saw such guilty faces. Paloma's mum jumped to her feet. David's dad put his head in his hands. The other two just stared as if an angel with a fiery sword was coming down the stairs.

"You never took them," David said. "I knew the carry-box hadn't been used. I knew it! It was all dusty!"

Paloma suddenly understood. She let out a scream.

"You didn't take them?" she cried. "Why not? Where are they? Where did you leave them?"

The two mothers rushed to the stairs. The two dads just stood there.

"Darlings, let us explain! We're terribly sorry! We didn't know what to do—" the mothers both burbled at once.

David stood absolutely still on the stairs.

"Where are they?" he asked in an almost grown-up voice.

"They are *all right*," said Paloma's dad, very loudly. "I'm absolutely sure of it. They'll find food for themselves, and when we get back, there they'll be." He told them what had happened, how the cats had disappeared, how they had to

pretend or the children would never have agreed to come to Wales.

"No, we wouldn't!" shouted Paloma. "Oh, poor Peony, poor little girl!" And she set up the loudest caterwaul any of them had ever heard. Well, you can't blame her.

Everyone talked at once, Paloma howled, David ran back up the stairs and shut himself in the bathroom so no one would see that *he* was crying too. It took half an hour to talk him into opening the door.

You can probably guess what the end was.

The children simply said they wanted to go home. And the parents couldn't think of any reason not to agree. The rest of the holiday would have been hopeless, anyway.

So the next day they packed up and drove home – a week early.

19. Where Are They?

The long journey home was strangely silent. Usually there were car games and everyone talked and played CDs or the radio. But this time it was different.

The children weren't talking to their parents due to anger. The parents weren't talking to each other due to shame. The

children, who rode together in the back of Paloma's car, weren't talking to each other either, because there was nothing to say. They each sat quiet in their own thoughts.

Paloma really had only one thought. Would the cats be there when they got back, and if so, what state would they be in after a week without any food? She could *feel* Peony's loneliness and hunger in her heart and her tummy.

David sat hugging his favourite cat book. Every now and then he opened it and read a bit. He read about feral cats, how they coped without families. Some feral cats had never had families to feed and shelter them. They were just like wild creatures. If kind people put food out for them, they might eat it, but they wouldn't let anyone touch them.

Maybe Turk would be like that – if he was there; if he hadn't run away for good. How could Turk ever love and trust him again after he'd gone off and left him? That's the trouble with animals. You can't explain things to them. You can't even say you're sorry.

The two cars arrived home at about the same time. The minute their car stopped, the two children jumped out. They stood on their doorsteps, waiting impatiently for the dads to open the front doors. As soon as they did, the children

rushed in, through their houses to the back doors, and out into their gardens.

It was evening. The sun was low. There was no sign of anything alive. Even the bird-table in David's garden was empty. It seemed to both the children that a kind of emptiness lay across the gardens, sad, like the long shadows made by the setting sun.

They both called and called.

"Turk!"

"Peony!"

Nothing.

Meanwhile Paloma's mother was ringing the next-door bell. The nicer neighbour came.

"Did you see the cats while we were away?" Paloma's mum asked eagerly.

She shook her head.

"I heard them meowing, and I called, but they never came."

"Oh... oh... This is awful!" Paloma's mum muttered, nearly crying. She turned away without even saying thank you.

The two mothers and the two fathers came out into the gardens to help call. But in the end they had to give up. The dads opened up the catflaps.

"Maybe they'll come back in the night. I'm sure they will," said David's dad.

David said nothing. He was quite sure they wouldn't. Why would they?

They must have tried to get in and bumped their heads on the catflaps that wouldn't open. Turk wasn't stupid. He wouldn't keep on bumping his head.

Next door Paloma was crying. Not caterwauling. It was too bad for that. She just lay on her bed surrounded by all her toy cats and tried to let them comfort her while her tears fell on them.

Her mum came.

"Darling. I'm so terribly sorry."

"Maybe she's dead."

"Dead! Oh, no, I'm sure she's not! She'll come back. She will. We must believe she will!"

Paloma cried herself to sleep. Her mum nearly did too. Her dad went out into the dark garden and called again, quietly. He felt like a criminal. He hadn't said a prayer for years, but now he did. "Please God, send our cat home."

20. Peony in a Mess

Peony wasn't dead. But she had got herself into a bad place.

It was because of the tree, the one leaning against the wall. By now she'd climbed it so often, it seemed the easiest thing in the world. So she thought climbing all trees was easy.

After the bin-men came and took the black sacks away, she and Turk had to go back to hunting. They didn't go out in the street any more, because that was where the fox was. But, just as the cats were now scared and wary of the fox, all the birds and other creatures were scared and wary of the cats. The birds didn't come down to the lawns or to sit on the garden furniture. They stayed high in the trees.

And Peony and Turk could hear them up there. Their songs sounded like jeering: "Cheep, cheep! You can't catch us!"

Then there were the squirrels. Squirrels did come down into the gardens if there was any food there, but they never went far from a tree. And they could shoot up a tree like an arrow. A few times Turk, lurking in the bushes, would pounce out

at a squirrel, but it would shoot out of reach in a flash, leaving Turk clinging to the bottom of the tree, furiously lashing his tail.

Peony, watching, thought she could do better.

She saw where one squirrel went – up a tree with smooth bark. Very tall. The first branches were far above her head – much higher than the wall. But two days after the bin-men took their food away, Peony was hungry. Very, very hungry.

She hid in some bushes at the foot of the squirrel's tree.

She kept very still, waiting.

At last, the squirrel came down its big tree into a garden where there was a bird-feeder full of nuts. The squirrel ran along a wire that crossed the garden and held up the bird-feeder. It tore the feeder

open to get at
the nuts, but most of
them fell out. The
squirrel ran back
along the wire, down
a post and onto the
ground to get them.

Peony had been
waiting for this! She
leapt out of her
hiding-place. The
squirrel saw her
coming. It dodged
her and fled up
the tree as easily
as if it were running

along the ground. Peony, with all her new-found speed and bravery, sprang after it.

This tree was not like her other tree. It was smoother. But she was so hungry she didn't notice. She protracted her claws and scrambled up and up, keeping the squirrel's tail in sight. She climbed and climbed, pushed by her need to catch the squirrel and eat it, every last bit of it.

Well, maybe she'd share with Turk. It was a big, fat squirrel; enough for two.

But – where was it?

Peony realised she'd lost sight of it. And she was high up in the branches of the tree. When she lay along a branch and looked down, she got a fright. She'd never been so high. Much, much higher than the wall. She could go head-first down the wall, but she couldn't do that now. It was too high and the tree was too smooth.

She began to meow for Turk. "Come and help me! Get me down! I'm frightened!"

21. Turk To The Rescue

And, three gardens away, Turk heard her.

He'd been stealing the food of the rotten dog. This dog liked to eat his food in his kennel which was out in his garden. A cat had to take a big risk to get it, but Turk waited till he knew the dog was off

somewhere with his person. Then he sneaked down to the kennel and was just helping himself to a nice bit of dog food when he heard Peony calling him.

He climbed up onto a shed and stood on the roof. He looked all round, his ears pricked. He was looking in the gardens, on the walls, on the sheds. She wasn't there.

He ran along the shed roof towards the sound of her voice. He jumped onto the top of a fence and ran along it. It was narrow and he nearly fell, but he got to a wall and ran along that. He was getting nearer. But where was she?

"I'm here! I'm here! Look up and see me and come for me!"

He saw her! But she was impossibly high. Turk knew he couldn't get her down. He didn't stop to think, to remember that

his family had gone. He raced for home.

David was making a Lego castle to take his mind off things when he heard – *the clack of the catflap.*

It was the best sound he'd ever heard.

He jumped up off the floor, his heart in his throat, and ran to the kitchen. And there he was! Turk! His beautiful Turk! – but changed. Thinner. His white fur marked with dirt and fights. David ran to him, picked him up, cuddled and kissed him, saying his name over and over again.

"Turk! Turk! My lovely, lovely Turk, you came back! You came back!" (Before you ask, yes, he was. Crying. No shame in that.)

Turk, as soon as he could, jumped to the floor and went back through the catflap.

"Turk! Don't go! Come back!"

David threw open the back door. Turk was standing there on the patio, waving his tail and looking straight at him. His blue eyes were fixed on him. But then he looked away and started to run down the garden.

He climbed on to the shed at the bottom. Then he disappeared into the garden that backed on to theirs. A minute later, David saw him on another shed roof, and then another wall, further away. A white shape, disappearing and

reappearing, getting smaller as he went into the distance.

David had stopped calling. He climbed on to a garden chair and then on to the picnic table. That way he could see further. He scanned the walls and shed roofs. And then he saw him! A little white shape.

Turk was standing still on a wall about four gardens away. David narrowed his eyes and stared as hard as he could. What was Turk doing?

He was staring upward. Over his head were the branches of a tall tree.

David didn't waste a moment. He jumped down, ran through the house, out the front door, into the street and up to Paloma's door. He rang their special ring. He rang it three times one after the other as hard as he could.

Ding... Ding-ding-diiiiiing!

Paloma came running. She threw open the door.

"I think I know where she is," said David. "Come quick!"

Getting Peony down from the tree, which was in a rather far-away neighbour's garden, wasn't easy. In the end they had to call the fire brigade.

Usually when the fire brigade is called for something that isn't a fire, they don't make a special noise driving through the streets, but this time they did. Probably because Paloma's dad had sounded so frantic over the phone, that they thought at the very least his house was burning down, possibly with him in it. So the red engine came roaring and blasting its siren and clanging its bell, and all the

neighbours came out to see where the fire was.

Luckily the tree was near a street wall and the firemen were able to run a ladder up it from the pavement. All the neighbours stood around staring upwards. When the fireman backed down the ladder, clear of the leaves, holding Peony in one arm, there was a mighty cheer that scared her so much she nearly bolted back up the tree again.

But the fireman hung on tight and brought her down, and handed her to Paloma.

"Oh... thank you! Thank you!" she cried, and kissed his belt, which was as high up him as she could reach. He went as red as the engine, patted her on the head, and the fire engine drove away while all the neighbours clapped. It was

the best show they'd seen all week; much better (and much more real) than reality TV.

Paloma, David, and Paloma's mum and dad went home with Peony and

made the biggest fuss of her that any cat has ever had. Made of her. Fuss. If you see what I mean. (I'm sorry. I'm a bit over-excited myself.)

And Turk? Well, of course Turk was the hero of the hour.

22. Peony Springs a Surprise

A few months after the Great Rescue, Peony disappeared.

Paloma was frantic. She hunted for her, and called for her in the garden. Her mum and dad looked too. They looked everywhere. But they couldn't find her.

Paloma was more grown up now. She hardly caterwauled any more. But it was hard not to cry when she came home from school every day and there was no Peony waiting for her. Had she gone forever?

And then, three days later, Peony showed up! She came streaking down the stairs, through the kitchen, and out through the catflap. The family looked at each other. Paloma felt happiness flowing through her like hot chocolate on a cold day.

"She's been in the house all the time!" said Paloma's dad.

"But where? Where's she been hiding?" asked Paloma.

Her mum said, "Don't try to catch her. Just watch where she goes."

After a little while Peony streaked

back in again. She gulped down some food and almost flew upstairs. Paloma followed her. Peony went into the spare room and shot under the bed.

Paloma lay down on the floor and peered into the darkness. No Peony! She'd disappeared! Where could she have gone?

Paloma wriggled her way under the bed on her tummy. Then she noticed. There was an old doll's cradle under there, in the corner. Well, I told you Paloma wasn't into dolls. Someone had given it to her ages ago and she'd never used it.

Now she reached into it. She touched something warm that moved. It wasn't Peony. It was lots of little soft balls of fur. All snuggled up together. And as she poked around, she heard noises.

Squeaks.

Paloma wriggled out backwards and ran downstairs.

"I've found her! And… I think…"

"Ah!" said her mum, with a big smile. "She's had her kittens!"

Paloma stared at her. "You knew?"

"Er – well, yes, that's why she got so fat."

"I thought she got fat because she'd been so thin! Why didn't you tell me?"

"It's a long time to wait. I thought it would be a nice surprise."

Paloma felt a thrill go down her back. "Can we see them?"

They all went upstairs and Dad very gently pulled the doll's cradle out from under the bed.

And sure enough, there in amongst the soft doll's blankets was Peony. And lying

close to her tummy were: one, two, three, four, five tiny kittens.

Two of them were black. Two were white. And one was black and white. Their eyes were closed and they had tiny pink mouths.

I won't try to tell you Paloma was happier than when she got Peony back

after thinking she'd lost her for ever. But she was very, very happy, just the same. Even when her mum and dad told her she mustn't – no, absolutely not – pick up any of the kittens yet. Or even touch them. (That was all they knew, because they hadn't read any cat books.)

You can guess the first person Paloma wanted to tell.

David's face lit up.

"How many?"

"Five. And two of them are white."

David felt almost as if he himself had just become a dad. He had that same proud grin on his face that new dads often have. They ran back to Paloma's house and up to the spare room.

Paloma put her finger to her lips. "We mustn't disturb them."

They sat on the floor and gazed into the doll's cradle.

"We should bring Turk to see them," Paloma whispered.

"I don't suppose he'd know they were his," David said. "Shall we think of names for them?"

"Yes! You name the white ones and I'll name the black ones."

David thought of the whitest things he knew. "What about School Shirt and Kleenex Tissue?"

Paloma laughed so much she rolled on her back, kicked her legs in the air, and showed her knickers. "That's the *silliest—*"

David said, "I was joking! Seriously. Let's call them Tipp-Ex and Shaving Foam."

Paloma hit him. Not hard.

"Well, you go."

Paloma still liked flower names. She said, "There are tulips that are nearly black. So Tulip. And as they're black, like witches' cats, I'll call the other one Black Magic. Madge for short."

"And what if they're toms?"

"Tango and Blackie. Now you. And no jokes!"

David said, "I don't want to have to change names when we find out if they're toms or queens. So I'll call mine Cloud and Snowy. That'll do, whatever they are."

That left the fifth kitten.

While they sat there thinking of something black and white, David reached into the cradle and lifted the black and white kitten. Paloma nearly screamed.

"You mustn't!"

"It says in the cat book you should *habituate* kittens by handling them when they're tiny."

"What's habituate mean?"

"Get them used to you, I think. Only don't take them out of the nest."

So then Paloma very gently curled her hand around one of the black kittens. Incredible softness, warmth, sweetness.

Peony narrowed her eyes and made a quiet, warning noise.

"OK, Peony, darling," said Paloma, and laid the kitten back with the others. "I was just habituating." It was good to have a fellow cat-fancier around who read serious books.

"Magpie!" David shouted suddenly.

Paloma looked at him. "That's it," she said. "That's it. That's the perfect name."

A few weeks after that, Paloma's family had three cats, and so did David's. I'm not going to tell you what the parents felt about this, but sometimes guilty feelings are useful.

Just a minute... Mother cat. Father cat. Plus two of the kittens in each house. (One black and one white, if you're interested.) Which adds up to six altogether.

But there were seven.

So what happened to the fifth kitten –

black and white Magpie?

That's another story. But I'll tell you the beginning of it. Magpie was the first of the kittens to crawl away from its mother and fall head-first out of the cradle. The first, a week later, to get lost and have the whole household hunting for it. The first, a few weeks after that, to find the catflap and venture out into the big world.

They never found it after that. But don't worry. There's an old story that David read to Paloma, about The Cat that Walks by Himself. The cat in the story is independent, proud, and very clever. And I think that story could have been written about Magpie.